D0065408

MATCH WITS WITH

SHERLOCK HOLMES
Volume 4

MATCH WITS
WITH
SHERLOCK HOLMES

The Adventure of the Copper Beeches

The Redheaded League

adapted by
MURRAY SHAW

from the original stories by Sir Arthur Conan Doyle

illustrated by **GEORGE OVERLIE**

Carolrhoda Books, Inc./Minneapolis

To young mystery lovers everywhere

The author gratefully acknowledges permission granted by Dame Jean Conan Doyle to use the Sherlock Holmes characters and stories created by Sir Arthur Conan Doyle.

Text copyright © 1990 by Murray Shaw.
Illustrations copyright © 1990 by Carolrhoda Books, Inc.

Library of Congress Cataloging-in-Publication Data

Shaw, Murray.
  Match wits with Sherlock Holmes. The Adventure of the Copper Beeches. The Redheaded League / adapted by Murray Shaw from the original stories by Sir Arthur Conan Doyle : illustrated by George Overlie.
      p.   cm. — (Match wits with Sherlock Holmes : v. 4)
  Summary: Presents two adventures of Sherlock Holmes and Dr. Watson, each accompanied by a section identifying the clues mentioned in the story and explaining the reasoning used by Holmes to put the clues together and come up with a solution. Also includes a map highlighting the sites of the mysteries.
  ISBN 0-87614-388-5
  1. Children's stories. English. [1. Mystery and detective stories. 2. Literary recreations.] I. Doyle. Arthur Conan. Sir, 1859-1920. II. Overlie, George, ill. III. Title. IV. Series: Shaw, Murray, Match wits with Sherlock Holmes : v. 4.
PZ7.S53426Co   1990
[Fic]—dc20   89-22294
                                                                CIP
                                                                 AC

Manufactured in the United States of America

1   2   3   4   5   6   7   8   9   10   99   98   97   96   95   94   93   92   91   90

CONTENTS

In the year 1887, Sir Arthur Conan Doyle created two characters who captured the imagination of mystery lovers around the world. They were Sherlock Holmes—the world's greatest fictional detective—and his devoted companion, Dr. John H. Watson. These characters have never grown old. For over a hundred years, they have delighted readers of all ages.

In the Sherlock Holmes stories, the time is always the late 1800s and the setting, Victorian England. Holmes and Watson live in London, on the second floor of 221 Baker Street. When Holmes travels through back alleys and down gaslit streets to solve crimes, Watson is often at his side. After Holmes's cases are complete, Watson records them. These are the stories of their adventures.

INTRODUCTION

When Watson first came to live at 221B Baker Street, he decided to put Holmes's skills to the test:

"Holmes," I remarked one day, "this watch has recently been given to me. Can you tell me something about its last owner?"

"I would be delighted to try, my dear Watson," said Holmes. He took the gold pocket watch from me and inspected it carefully.

"First," he began casually, "The W. engraved on the watch's back would be Watson, and since the make of this watch is fifty years old, I would say this was your father's watch first. And since jewelry is generally passed from father to eldest son, I would assume this last belonged to your older brother."

"Quite so. Anything else?"

"Your brother was an untidy man who was rather careless. For much of his life, he went back and forth between poverty and riches."

"Holmes, this is cruel," I said, taken aback. "You have researched my family, and this is a strange joke."

Holmes looked up, astonished. "My dear doctor, I meant no offense. Truly, I have deduced these things from the watch alone. Let me show you." He handed me the magnifying glass.

"You see, Watson, the watch case is dented and has a series of cuts. Clearly, the watch was carelessly kept in the same pocket as keys and coins. And because the watch is of high quality, it is reasonable to assume that your brother had been left with some good prospects."

"Yes, I can see those things," I admitted.

"Now, Watson, look at the inside of the case. Pawnbrokers often scratch ticket numbers on pawned objects. This watch has at least four sets of numbers. Obviously, your brother would sell the watch for quick money and later pay to have it back."

I shook his hand. "Please accept my apologies, Holmes. Once you reveal your methods, things are as clear as daylight." As usual, Holmes had proven what a master detective he is.

"'First, I must say that I've not been
ill-treated by the Rucastles.'"

THE ADVENTURE OF
THE COPPER BEECHES

rising one spring morning later than usual, I was not surprised to find Holmes already awake. He was sitting comfortably in his favorite armchair near the hearth. Numerous pages of the morning newspapers were stacked next to him, and he was presently bent over the columns of *The Daily Chronicle.*

"Good morning, Watson," he called, turning the page. "The criminal mind has lost all originality," he said bitterly. "I've looked through all the morning papers, and there's not a sign of an unusual crime. My practice is fated to become an agency for finding lost hats and advising the bewildered."

"Holmes," I said, "it can't be as bad as all that. Besides, isn't it a good thing for society that crimes are becoming less common?"

Holmes picked up the cinder tongs and selected an ember from what was left of last night's blaze. With it he lit his long cherrywood pipe, which he often smoked when he was in the mood for discussion.

"My dear Watson," he said after a few thoughtful puffs, "crimes aren't less common in occurrence; they are simply more common in design. When I'm reduced to advising young ladies just out of their boarding schools, I've surely hit bottom in my profession. The letter I received this morning marks my zero point. Here, read it!"

Holmes tossed me a crumpled note.

My dear Mr. Holmes,
   I am very anxious for your advice as to whether
or not I should accept a governess position that
has been offered to me. I shall call at half-past
ten tomorrow if it is not an inconvenience.
                              Yours faithfully,
                              Violet Hunter

"Do you know her?" I asked.

"I certainly do not," replied Holmes as the doorbell rang. "That, however, must be her." He rose to answer the door.

Inside stepped a neatly dressed young lady with long, striking chestnut hair, a bright, fresh face, and a sprinkling of freckles. She walked in confidently, like someone used to making her own way in the world.

"Please excuse my troubling you, Mr. Holmes," she said politely, "I'm Miss Hunter. I've had a strange experience, and since I have no one else to guide me, I thought you might be able to help."

"Do sit down, Miss Hunter," Holmes said graciously. "I would be pleased to do what I can. This is my friend Dr. Watson, who often assists me."

I nodded to her from my place near the mantle. I could see that Holmes was impressed with Miss Hunter's manner and appearance. Settling back into his chair, he asked her to explain her situation.

"For the past five years," she began, "I was a

governess for Colonel Spence-Munro. Recently, however, he and his family moved to Halifax, Nova Scotia, and I was forced to seek new employment. Since newspaper advertisements brought me no prospects, I went to an employment agency called Westaways, run by a Miss Stoper.

"One day, when I entered Miss Stoper's office, I found her talking with a short, stout man. When he saw me, he sprang to his feet and exclaimed, 'Indeed, this is she! I could not ask for anyone better!' He smiled pleasantly and complimented me on my professional appearance. Then he asked me if I would consider a position taking care of his six-year-old son.

"I was relieved to be asked about a position," continued Miss Hunter, "so I said that I would consider it. When I told him that I had made four pounds a month at my last position, he cried, 'My, that's a mere pittance for someone of your qualities. You will be responsible for the education of a child. That surely is worth at least a hundred pounds a year.'

"Naturally, Mr. Holmes," Miss Hunter said shyly, "I was both surprised and pleased by the generosity of his offer. I have never run into such consideration. But I also felt uneasy that he should be willing to pay so much to hire me when he knew so little about me. So I asked him what my duties would be.

"'You will have just one dear little boy to mind,' he answered me proudly, 'and a real romper he is. You should see him kill cockroaches. Smack! Smack! Smack! Three are gone before you know it.'"

Holmes and I looked at each other with distaste. She said, "Of course, I was put off by this child's odd form of amusement, but I thought his father must be joking. When I asked him if the child would be my only duty, he replied cautiously, 'No, not quite. My wife often amuses herself with styles and fads. She may ask you to wear a dress she will give to you, or to sit here rather than there, or to cut your hair.'

"As you can imagine," Miss Hunter said, "I was shocked at his last request. It has taken me a long time to grow my hair to such a length, and I did not want to cut it off to suit a small whim of his wife's. So I told him that I could agree to the other things, but cutting my hair was out of the question.

"At this, the man looked disappointed. 'Are you sure you won't reconsider?' he asked me. He added in a coaxing tone, 'We live at the Copper Beeches in Hampshire, near Winchester. It's really quite lovely.'

"When I shook my head, he shrugged his shoulders and said, 'Well then, Miss Stoper, I must continue to look for someone else.' Then Miss Stoper looked at me with pursed lips and said, 'Sensible women do not value their vanity over a position. There is little sense in keeping you on our list if you must be *so* particular.'"

Miss Hunter went on wearily, "Once I returned home, I found several unpaid bills and began to wonder if Miss Stoper was right. By the next day, I felt quite sure of it. Then this note arrived, posted from the Copper Beeches."

She handed the note to Holmes, and he read:

Dear Miss Hunter,
   My wife is very anxious for you to come.
We'd be glad to provide you with one hundred and
twenty pounds a year to make up for the loss
of your hair.
   Please do come. I will meet you at the station.
             Faithfully yours,
             Jephro Rucastle

"Mr. Holmes," she said, "I have nearly decided to accept the position. But before I send a telegram to Mr. Rucastle and have my hair cut, I thought it would be wise to have your opinion."

"Well, Miss Hunter," said Holmes, "if you've made your decision, there is nothing to say. However, it's not a position I would like a sister of mine to accept. Mr. Rucastle seems a bit too eager and too generous."

"What could be his meaning, Mr. Holmes?" she asked.

"Miss Hunter, I am at a loss since I have no data on Mr. Rucastle's background. You have met the man— what do you think of his character?"

"Well, he seems pleasant enough from appearances. Perhaps his wife is insane, or nearly so, and that is why he wants to give in to her unusual demands."

Holmes looked at her approvingly. "That seems the most logical conclusion. However, if you should be in any danger . . ."

"Danger!" Miss Hunter's hazel eyes opened wide.

"Pray, be calm. I foresee no specific danger, but you must be careful. If you need us day or night, do not hesitate to contact us."

"Mr. Holmes, Dr. Watson," she said, rising and offering us each her hand in turn, "you are both very kind. I am more at ease knowing that I can turn to you if I must."

She then wished us a good day and left.

"Well," I said to Holmes, "she seems to be a woman who can watch over herself."

Holmes was leaning on his elbow, his forehead creased in thought. "Yes, indeed, but I doubt a month will go by without word from her."

———— ⚬ ————

Three weeks later a telegram arrived, just as Holmes had predicted. We had both risen early and were sitting down to breakfast. He read the brief message aloud:

*Please be at the Black Swan Hotel in Winchester
at midday. Do come! I'm at my wit's end.*
                    HUNTER

"If we hurry," I said, "we can catch the train and make it to Winchester by eleven-thirty."

Holmes threw his napkin down and rose. "A pity to waste a good breakfast," he said, "but there's no help for it."

———— ⚬ ————

Once on the train, we watched the gentle green hills

pass by, crisscrossed by hedges and dotted with farms. I opened the window to breathe in the exhilarating scents of spring.

"Ah, Holmes," I said with enthusiasm, "doesn't it do your heart good to see the freshness of it all after the smoke and fog of London?"

Surprisingly, Holmes was grave. "My dear Watson, looks can deceive. I fear that many a crime has gone undetected in these lonely little homesteads."

"What?" I said, astounded. "Is your mind so filled with crime that you can't enjoy a day in the country?"

"No, Watson," he said pondering, "it's the loneliness out here. Who is there to hear a scream or a cry for help? If Miss Hunter were in London, I would not worry for her safety nearly as much as I do."

"But, Holmes," I protested, "Miss Hunter is not being held captive if she can meet us in town."

"Quite so. But we will wait for further information before we draw any conclusions."

The town's cathedral soon came into view, and within a quarter of an hour, we had found our way to the Black Swan Hotel in the middle of High Street. Miss Hunter had engaged a sitting room and was waiting inside with lunch for us.

"Oh, it's so good of you to come," she said, rising to meet us. Her face looked even younger now that her shining locks had been cropped to small rings around her face.

"The Rucastles are so strange," she said, "that I've been trying to decide if I should stay or go."

"Pray, tell us what has happened," Holmes said, removing his hat and getting straight to business.

"I must be quick," she said, speaking rapidly. "I promised Mr. Rucastle I'd be back by three. First, I must say that I've not been ill-treated by the Rucastles. Mrs. Rucastle is a silent woman who seems to care only for Mr. Rucastle and their son. Her husband treats her kindly enough in a laughing way, and they seem to be a happy couple. She is his second wife and is fifteen years younger than he is. Mr. Rucastle was a widower when they met, and he has one daughter, Alice, from his first marriage. From what I have gathered, Alice is in her twenties and has moved away to live with an aunt because she does not get along with her father's new wife."

"That is not strictly unheard of," said Holmes.

"No, certainly not," she agreed. "And Mrs. Rucastle seems perfectly sane, but sometimes I'll catch her sitting by herself and crying softly."

"Is there a reason for her tears?" Holmes inquired.

Miss Hunter shook her head. "None that I know of. Maybe she is crying for her child—he is a spoiled, ill-natured creature. He delights in hurting things smaller than himself, such as mice, birds, and small insects."

"A terrible trait in one so young," I said.

Miss Hunter looked at me sadly. "How true! I'm doing my best to distract him, but it does no good. The Rucastles' servants, Mr. and Mrs. Toller, are unappealing as well. Mr. Toller is moody and walks about smelling of liquor. Twice I have seen him very drunk, but no one else seems to notice. And Mrs. Toller just keeps to herself.

"On top of it all, Mr. Rucastle has a huge, vicious dog, named Carlo," she added grimly. "It's a mastiff, and he uses it to watch the grounds at night. The dog is fed only rarely so it will stay 'keen as mustard,' as Mr. Rucastle says." As Holmes listened, he ate slowly and stared grimly at the far wall.

"Now to the heart of the matter," she continued. "One day shortly after my arrival, Mr. Rucastle suggested I put a dress on that had been laid out on my bed. He explained that his wife has a special liking for the dress's particular shade of blue, especially against the unusual shade of my hair. The dress showed signs of wear, but it fit me exactly, and when I came down the stairs in it, they were delighted.

"Now the Rucastle's home is set on the main road from the village, near a stand of copper beech trees. Their front parlor has three long windows that face the road and reach almost to the floor. On this day the Rucastles asked me to sit in a chair next to the windows with my back to the road. Then Mr. Rucastle began entertaining his wife and me with funny stories, puffing out his chest as he played different characters. I laughed heartily at his performance, but his wife just sat on the sofa with her hands in her lap. After a while Mr. Rucastle got tired and suggested I change clothes to check on his son."

"Did this happen more than once?" asked Holmes.

"Yes," Miss Hunter said. "Two days later Mr. Rucastle again asked me to put on the dress. Only this time, after telling us stories, Mr. Rucastle gave me a novel and asked me to read to them. I did, but abruptly, in the middle of a sentence, he told me that they had heard enough. Then he sent me back to the nursery. Over the next week, this happened a few more times, sometimes in the morning, sometimes in the afternoon. Each time I became more curious to know what was happening on the road behind me."

"This information does seem crucial," said Holmes, now finished with his meal and sitting back with his fingertips pressed together.

Miss Hunter smiled, happy to have pleased Holmes.

"So I devised a method. One day I took a sliver of glass that had broken out of my hand mirror and hid it in my handkerchief. That morning, when Mr. Rucastle made me laugh, I put the handkerchief to my face as if to dry my watering eyes. I did this a few times. At first I didn't notice anything in the mirror. Then I spotted a young man leaning on a tree, staring at my back.

"At that point Mrs. Rucastle must have suspected that I had somehow seen what was behind me. She turned to her husband and said, 'Jephro, there is a young man out on the road, staring at Miss Hunter. Please send him away.' Mr. Rucastle then looked at me and demanded, 'Do you have a friend in these parts?' I replied that I did not. 'Then motion the man away,' he ordered. 'We'll have no young men sitting out there watching for you.' As I turned to wave the man away, Mr. Rucastle pulled the shade down. Since then he hasn't asked me to wear the blue dress."

"Have other strange things occurred?" asked Holmes.

Miss Hunter shivered slightly in her chair. "Yes," she said. "There is an old chest of drawers in the corner of my room. I had put some of my clothing into the top two drawers, but the third one was locked. So one evening I tried to unlock the drawer with some of the house keys the Rucastles had given me. One of them worked. When I opened the drawer, I was astonished by what I saw. Inside was the coil of hair I had saved from my haircut in London. I was confused. How could my hair possibly have come to be in this locked drawer?

"Trembling, I opened my trunk and there, in the bottom, was my coil of hair, just where I had left it. So whose hair was this? I wondered. I compared the two coils, and they were identical. I tried to think of an explanation but failed. And since I opened the drawer without the Rucastles' permission, I cannot ask them about it. So I must leave that mystery for you, Mr. Holmes."

"It may be a simple one, Miss Hunter," said Holmes, "but we'd better hear the rest of your tale before we draw any conclusions."

"Well, after I had been in the house a week," she went on, trying not to forget anything of importance, "I realized there were rooms next to the Tollers' section that were not being used. From the outside all that could be seen of the rooms were two dirty windows and a third window that was shuttered up. One day I saw Mr. Rucastle coming out of the unused hallway. This was not the smiling, jolly man I knew. His face was red with anger. He locked the door securely behind himself and brushed past me without a word. Later he apologized for his rudeness."

"Did he offer an explanation?" Holmes inquired.

"Yes. He said that he had a small laboratory in that section and an experiment had not worked as he had wished. He seemed to be telling the truth, but that wing still seemed mysterious to me. So I began to look for a chance to enter this forbidden area. From time to time, Mr. Toller checks these rooms and comes out carrying a black linen bag. Yesterday afternoon, when I came upstairs, I found he had forgotten the key in the door. No one was around so I slipped past the open door and into the hall.

"The passageway was narrow, with no wallpaper or carpet. I walked to the end of it, where there were three doors. Two were open, and I looked into the rooms behind them—they were dusty and deserted. The middle door, which belonged to the room with the shuttered window, was blocked by an iron bar and padlocked shut. As I peered through the slit between the door and the frame, something passed in front of the door. I was suddenly terrified. I turned and ran— ran as if a dreadful hand were going to clutch at me from behind. I rushed straight down the hall and out the door, right into the arms of Mr. Rucastle, who was waiting outside the door.

"'So it was you who was in the hall,' he said, half smiling. 'Why were you running, my dear young lady?' I told him that I'd been frightened by the darkness, and he asked sweetly, 'Is that all that frightened you?' When I nodded, he suddenly turned fierce and said harshly, 'You have good reason to be afraid, Missy. If I find you in there again, I'll throw you to the dog!' I was so startled that I pulled away and ran back to my room as fast as I could. That's when I decided to send you the telegram."

"You did the right thing, Miss Hunter," said Holmes, his long face stern. Then he rose from the table and began to pace. "Do you think Mr. Toller will be drunk this evening?" he asked.

"Yes," said Miss Hunter, surprised by his question, "I heard his wife say this morning that he was already drunk and no help at all."

"That's good," said Holmes. "Will the Rucastles be at home tonight?"

"No. They are going out for a visit and that is why I must be home by three—to look after the child."

"That's another thing in our favor," said Holmes. "And the wine cellar, does it have a good, strong lock?"

"Why, yes," she answered, still puzzled. I too was wondering what kind of plan Holmes was hatching and what he suspected.

"Can you do one thing for me, Miss Hunter?" Holmes asked gently.

"Why, of course, Mr. Holmes."

"Watson and I will be at the Copper Beeches by seven tonight. Could you get Mrs. Toller to go into the wine cellar and then lock her in? If you can, I think we can get to the heart of this mystery."

Miss Hunter rose, pulling herself to her full height. "I will be glad to do it."

—— ∽ ——

We arrived at the Copper Beeches promptly at seven. The gnarled old trees, with their red leaves shining in the setting sun, marked the Rucastle home. Miss Hunter was standing on the front steps waiting for us.

"Is Mrs. Toller locked up?" asked Holmes as we walked in. A loud thumping noise from downstairs answered his question.

The flush of excitement had made Miss Hunter's face almost as bright as her hair. "Mr. Toller is snoring on the kitchen rug, and I was able to sneak Mr. Rucastle's keys from his desk drawer. I've also locked that miserable child in his room, where I trust he will do no harm, at least for a little while."

"You have done admirably well, Miss Hunter. Be quick now and lead us to the forbidden wing."

We went up the back stairs to the locked door. Finding the right key, we went through the narrow, dusty passage to its end. All was silent. Holmes's face grew grim as he peered into the middle room through the slit of light at the edge of the door. "I hope we are not too late already."

We removed the bar but could not undo the lock. So, putting our shoulders to the door, we shoved hard until, with a loud crack, it gave way at the hinges. But the room was empty. Above us a skylight hung open.

"The villain must have carried her off through the skylight," said Holmes, jumping onto the table under the skylight and pulling himself to the roof. "There's a ladder under the eaves," he called out as he climbed back into the room. "Obviously, Mr. Rucastle guessed your intentions and has taken Alice off."

"His daughter?" Miss Hunter asked, astonished.

"Yes."

"But, Mr. Holmes," protested Miss Hunter, "the ladder was not there when the Rucastles left."

"He is a clever man, Miss Hunter. He must have returned while we were inside. I suspect those are his footsteps now. Your pistol, Watson."

We took a few steps back from the door, and suddenly a fat man strode into the room, ready to strike at us with a heavy stick. Miss Hunter screamed and fell back against the wall. "What have you done with your daughter?" Holmes demanded.

Mr. Rucastle cried out, "You thieves! You spies!" Then, seeing my pistol, he shrieked, "I know how to deal with you." He turned and clattered down the hall.

"He's going for Carlo," screamed Miss Hunter.

"Then we've got to lock the front door before he returns," said Holmes, rushing down the passage.

We made it to the stairs when we heard Carlo's loud, excited barking and then a scream of terror and agony. Within seconds an elderly man tottered out of the kitchen, squinting and swaying. It was the drunk Mr. Toller.

"In heaven's name, who loosed the dog?," he cried out, reeling against the wall. "Carlo's not been fed for days. Someone be quick, or it will be too late."

Holmes and I rushed out around the house and found a huge black dog on top of Rucastle, his teeth deep in the man's throat. The mastiff was snarling viciously, not loosening his grip until I shot him dead.

We quickly pulled the heavy animal off Rucastle, who was mangled and losing blood. He was barely alive as we carried him to the house. Mr. Toller went to get a doctor, and we let Mrs. Toller out of the cellar.

"A fine mess this is," Mrs. Toller said, taking charge. She pushed her gray hair back from her face and wrung water from the cloth she was using to tend Rucastle's wounds. "I wish the young miss would have told me of your plans instead of locking me in the cellar. Miss Alice has already escaped, and I want you all to remember I was the friend that stood by the girl."

"Pray, tell us what you know," said Holmes.

After wrapping Rucastle's bandages tight and making him as comfortable as she could, she pulled us out into the kitchen to tell her story.

"She was never happy at home, Miss Alice wasn't,"
Mrs. Toller began, "from the time her father married
again. But things got even worse for Miss Alice after
she met Mr. Fowler at a party and he started to come
calling for her. Near as I can tell, the young lass had
money coming to her from her mother's will. The
money was left in her father's name all the time she
was growing up. But when Mr. Fowler came courting
for Miss Alice, Mr. Rucastle started worrying about
that money. He tried to force her to sign the money
away to him. When Miss Alice turned stubborn and
wouldn't listen to him, he kept on worrying her till
she got brain fever. For six weeks she lay at death's
door, the poor thing did, and her beautiful hair had
to be cut off. Finally, she came out of it, weak and
pale. And through it all, Mr. Fowler stayed as true
to her as any man can be."

Holmes broke in. "So Mr. Rucastle imprisoned her
in the wing and kept Carlo on prowl at night."

"'Tis true," Mrs. Toller said.

"And he brought Miss Hunter from London to act
like Alice and send Mr. Fowler away for good."

"That was it, sir. And Mrs. Rucastle was none too
happy about it. She was worried they'd get caught.
She'd cry her eyes out, but did she lift a finger to help
Miss Alice? Not on your life!"

Holmes nodded, glad to have the full story told.
"Well, Mrs. Toller, I'm happy to see that Mr. Fowler
was such a persistent gentleman and that he found
help in you. I suspect that he came up to you at the

market one day and asked you to let him know when the Rucastles would be away."

"That he did, sir," she said, proud of herself. "Mr. Fowler is a kind gentleman—generous to those who help him. I did him right by taking care of my husband and the dog, and by putting out the ladder. All the rest was left to him."

"Mrs. Toller," said Holmes politely, "we beg your pardon for keeping you detained in the cellar. And we give you thanks for clearing up all the remaining details."

Just then the country doctor arrived, and Mrs. Rucastle was delivered home by some friends. Holmes and I led Miss Hunter out of the room to spare her further distress.

Later we heard that Mr. Rucastle survived the accident but was a broken man, needing constant nursing by his wife. Alice and Jason Fowler married and settled down to live in a nearby village. As for Violet Hunter, she eventually formed her own boarding school, where she met with great success.

And thus ended the unusual story of the Copper Beeches.

At the Copper Beeches, things were not as they seemed, even from the beginning. How did Holmes figure out that it was Alice in the wing and her lover on the street? It was a prime example of deductive reasoning. Look back over the case and find the facts, and then check the **CLUES** *to see how Holmes put them all together.*

CLUES
that led to the solution of
The Adventure of the Copper Beeches

Mr. Rucastle's decision to hire Miss Hunter based only on her appearance made Holmes suspicious of the man's intentions. Since Mr. Rucastle was also willing to pay Miss Hunter so much above the normal wage, Holmes became even more concerned.

Holmes was also disturbed by the cruel play of Mr. Rucastle's child. Holmes had often noticed that you can tell quite a bit about parents by looking at their children. Thus, Holmes felt that Mr. Rucastle was probably not the pleasant man he appeared to be. Another clue to Mr. Rucastle's true nature was his treatment of the dog—his cruel starving of the animal to make it vicious.

Since Mr. Rucastle asked Miss Hunter to cut off her hair, wear a worn blue dress, and sit by the windows, Holmes figured that Mr. Rucastle wanted her to look like someone else. This suspicion was confirmed when Miss Hunter said that she had found a coil of hair that looked just like her own. Holmes suspected that it had once belonged to the woman she was imitating. Who was this woman? It had to be someone who had once lived in the house—and that could only be Alice Rucastle.

Because Miss Hunter had to wear the dress in front of the windows, Holmes was sure that the performance was done so someone outside the house could see it. Who could it be? The young man was the next clue. Holmes assumed that the stranger on the front road was a friend of Alice's who was hoping to see her. Holmes also figured that Mr. Rucastle had Carlo put out at night to keep this man away from his daughter.

The final questions were: Why did the Rucastles want to pretend that Alice was still living there? Had they killed her? Had they sent her away? Holmes suspected that the answers to these questions were to be found in the forbidden wing. He thought it was likely that the Rucastles were holding Alice hostage in the wing and that they were doing it for money. Mrs. Toller's explanation of Alice's inheritance confirmed this theory.

"Suddenly, he plunged his hand deep
into the thickest part of my hair...."

THE REDHEADED LEAGUE

One fall day I returned to Baker Street to find Holmes in deep conversation with a stout man with blazing red hair. Not wishing to interrupt, I started for the door, but Holmes called out to me.

"It's not necessary for you to leave, Watson. I may need your assistance." Holmes nodded toward his visitor. "This is Mr. Jabez Wilson. He runs a small pawnbroker's shop on Saxe-Coburg Square. Mr. Wilson, this is Dr. Watson. He has been my partner on many successful occasions and has a deep interest in bizarre cases of this sort."

The heavy man raised himself from his chair and gave me a polite nod.

"Mr. Wilson," said Holmes, "would you mind telling your story to Dr. Watson? It is indeed very strange. And as you speak, I hope to detect whether or not an actual crime has been committed." Holmes sat comfortably in his armchair, with his fingertips pressed together, ready to listen carefully.

"Certainly," the portly man replied. He took out an old newspaper and spread it across his lap. His worn coat was unbuttoned to reveal a drab waistcoat and a heavy brass watch chain. He adjusted his spectacles. "Here it is," he said, pointing a grubby finger at the cramped newspaper column. "This is what started it all.

It's an advertisement that ran about two months ago."

He handed the newspaper to me, and I read:

FROM THE REDHEADED LEAGUE
There is an immediate opening for a league mem-
ber. Will receive four pounds a week for minor
services. All redheaded men who are of sound
body and mind may apply. Come in person on
Monday at eleven o'clock to the league's office—
7, Pope's Court, Fleet Street.

"What in heaven's name can this mean?" I exclaimed after reading it twice.

Holmes chuckled. "That is part of the mystery, my dear Watson. This is a refreshingly unusual case. Now, Mr. Wilson, would you tell us about yourself, your business, and how this advertisement affected you?"

"I run a small pawnshop on the lower floor of my home," said Mr. Wilson. "Lately, business has been poor, so I have worked with the assistance of just one clerk. This man, however, has been a blessing. He works for half the usual wages just to learn the trade."

"A most extraordinary find," I noted. "What is your clerk's name?"

"Vincent Spaulding," Wilson answered, "and I doubt a more efficient clerk could be found anywhere. The fellow does have his faults though. He is interested in photography, and he is always snapping pictures. Then he dives down into the cellar, like a rabbit into a hole, to develop them. But I allow him to continue this practice since I pay him so little."

"How old is this assistant?" asked Holmes.

"Only a little over thirty," Wilson replied. "He is very smart. One day he said to me, 'How I wish I were a redheaded man!' I laughed at him and asked him why. He told me that the Redheaded League has easy posts with good money, and it just happened to have an opening. Then he showed me the advertisement. Well, let me tell you, four pounds a week for light work seems a princely sum. I thought it was a kind of joke, but my clerk thought otherwise. He said that he has known of others who have found an easy living through the Redheaded League. He explained that an eccentric redheaded millionaire in America had died without heirs and left a will saying that he wanted to leave his money to others with the same hair color. Mr. Spaulding felt that since I had such striking red hair, I should surely apply."

Mr. Wilson undid one of the buttons on his waistcoat so he could breath easier. "I had my doubts at first, but my clerk persuaded me to close up shop and go with him to see what was happening in Fleet Street. Never was there such a sight! Pope's Court was filled from one end to the other with redheaded men. Every shade of red hair was there—straw, lemon, orange, brick, Irish setter, liver, and clay. But, I must say, very few had the fiery color I have. Somehow, and I'm not exactly sure how, my clerk managed to push and pull me through the crowd so we could make it to the front and into the office.

"Inside the office was a man with a head of hair even redder than mine. When we walked in, he sighed in relief. 'Ah, that's the perfect shade,' he said. He sent away the man in front of him and walked up to greet us. He introduced himself as Mr. Duncan Ross, field manager for the league. Then he walked slowly around me, his head cocked, looking at my hair. Suddenly, he plunged his hand deep into the thickest part of my hair and tugged on it until my eyes watered. I cried out in pain, but he just laughed. 'You must excuse me,' he said, 'but we must take precautions. We've been fooled by wigs and paint before.'"

Wilson frowned as Holmes and I struggled to hide our amusement. "Well," he continued, "Mr. Ross found me well suited for the position in all ways but one. By the rules of the league, all applicants should be married and able to produce more redheaded members. Since I am a bachelor, I should have been ruled out. Mr. Ross, though, found the color of my hair so ideal that he decided to make an exception." Wilson coughed and added humbly, "I do suspect, gentlemen, that he was tired of seeing applicants."

"At any rate," Wilson continued, "I was selected. The position required that I be in the office each day from 10:00 a.m. to 2:00 p.m., Monday through Friday. This was suitable for me, because quite often my business is slow during these hours. I knew Spaulding could easily look after the shop while I was gone.

"My duties for the league were simple. I was to

copy each volume of the *Encyclopaedia Britannica* with my own ink, pens, and blotting paper. Under no circumstances was I to leave the office during my work hours. If I did, I would lose the post immediately.

"I could hardly believe my good fortune," Wilson went on. "I set to work on my new job the next day, beginning with the letter *A*. Mr. Ross got me started and then checked on me occasionally. At two o'clock he complimented me on my work and sent me on my way. The rest of the week continued in the same fashion, and on Saturday Mr. Ross placed four gold coins down on my desk for the week's work." Wilson smiled, proud of the deal he had made.

"As the weeks went on," Wilson said, "Mr. Ross trusted me more, checking on me less and less. Eight weeks later I had made it through *Abbots, Architecture,* and *Armour.* I was quite looking forward to the letter *B* when everything suddenly came to a halt. One morning I arrived at the office and found this note tacked on the door."

He unfolded a note and handed it to Holmes. It read:

THE REDHEADED LEAGUE IS DISSOLVED.
OCTOBER 9, 1890

Wilson paused to let us ponder this turn of events. It all struck us as so strange that we started to chuckle.

"This may sound humorous, but indeed it is not," said Wilson, a little insulted. "It is a loss of four pounds a week for me, and that is no small amount."

Holmes straightened up in his chair and stopped smiling. "I do agree, Mr. Wilson. Pray, continue."

"I was stunned, as you can imagine. I went to the owner of the house, but he claimed that he knew of no such person as Mr. Duncan Ross. He said that the redhaired man who had rented the office was a Mr. William Morris, an accountant. He had moved to 17 King Edward Street. I hurried to that address as quickly as I could, but it turned out to be the office of a company making artificial kneecaps."

"So how did you proceed?" asked Holmes.

"I was at my wit's end. My clerk tried to assure me that all will be well. He thinks that I will most likely hear from Mr. Ross soon, but I am not so sure. I had heard that you are kind to poor folk, so I came to you as quickly as possible."

"A wise choice, Mr. Wilson," said Holmes, leaning back into his chair once more. "This is an unusual case, and I think more is at stake than just a loss of four pounds a week. This assistant of yours, how long has he been with you?"

"Nearly three months. I ran an advertisement, and to be quite honest, I hired him because he was willing to work for less than the others who applied."

"Ah," said Holmes thoughtfully, "and what does he look like?"

"He is slim and moves with amazing quickness around the shop. He is of average height, clean shaven, and has a small, round white scar on his forehead. It looks like an acid burn."

Holmes sat up alertly. "Did you notice, by chance, if his ears are pierced?"

"Why, yes, now that you mention it, they are. I thought it odd and certainly uncommon."

"Is this man still working for you?"

"Oh, yes. I have grown to depend upon him. In fact, I must soon return to assist him. Do you think, Mr. Holmes, that you can find out why the league was dissolved? It seems a cruel prank to me."

"I understand your concerns," said Holmes. "As this is Saturday, I expect to have an answer for you by Monday." With that, we wished the crestfallen Wilson a good afternoon.

———— ✎ ————

After Wilson left, Holmes leaned back in his chair. "Watson," he said, "I have often found that the cases that are made up of ordinary events are the most difficult. The everyday details make the extraordinary ones hard to see. I think I'll have to sit and consider this particular case."

Then he lit his black clay pipe and pulled his knees to his chest. He remained that way for such a long time that I began to think he had fallen asleep. But suddenly, he jumped to his feet. His eyes were sparkling.

"Watson, I suspect we're dealing with a very clever and dangerous man. Wilson's description of his clerk sounds very much like that of a criminal the police department has been trying to catch for years. I think I know what he is up to, but before I will know for sure, I have to check one or two things. Would you like to accompany me to Saxe-Coburg Square?"

"Of course," I said, "I wouldn't miss the investigation of such a strange matter." So we took our topcoats, hats, and canes and went off to hail a cab.

———— ∽ ————

In a short while, we arrived at the small square. It was a plot of weedy grass, enclosed by a railing and a gate. Shabby two-story houses of brick lined its four sides, and a heavy smell of smoke and soot hung around them. Many had shops on the lower floors.

Over the door of one of the houses were three faded gold balls and a wooden sign saying *JABEZ WILSON.*

Holmes approached the pawn shop and then walked up the street, peering at the buildings. When he reached the corner, he retraced his steps. As he neared the pawnshop entrance, he gave a few sharp raps on the pavement with his walking stick. I watched this little ritual with puzzled amusement. The pavement was old and dirty, but it sounded solid, not needing repair. Holmes smiled and rang the bell.

The door was opened by the clerk Wilson had described.

"I say, good fellow," said Holmes in his social voice, "could you direct me to the Strand?"

"Indeed," said the man in a clipped, crisp voice, "take the third right and fourth left." Then he quickly closed the door.

"Smart fellow," Holmes said as we walked away. "One of the smartest in London."

"I don't understand, Holmes. Don't you want to ask him about the Redheaded League?"

"He's given me all the information I need." Holmes replied. "Did you notice the wrinkles and stains on the knees of his trousers?"

"Why, no, but . . ."

"No buts, Watson. Come, let us see what is behind Saxe-Coburg Square."

Holmes turned the corner and walked to the neighborhood behind the square. It was bustling with activity, unlike the quiet, forlorn little area we had just left. Here people were constantly passing, and a steady stream of carriages and cabs was moving in both directions. Holmes carefully observed the buildings that were on either side of the busy street.

"My good doctor," he said, "it's an important habit of the mind to observe all things in their exact and precise order. For instance, we have on our side of the street a little newspaper shop, Mortimer's Tobacco, the City and Suburban Bank, an Indian restaurant, and a carriage stop. Such details may prove to be extremely important."

He turned and started walking to Saxe-Coburg Square. I followed him. "You see," he continued, "we are spies in enemy territory, and we are playing a game for large stakes." He paused and turned to look at me. "Are you ready for some high adventure?"

"Why, certainly," I said, catching the pitch of excitement in his voice.

"Then meet me at Baker Street at ten o'clock. And please remember to bring your revolver. It may turn out to be quite necessary. Until then, farewell. I have a few things yet to attend to." He hailed a cab and left me pondering the whole situation. How could copying pages out of the *Encyclopaedia Britannica* lead to dangerous adventure? Where were we going tonight, and who were we fated to meet?

—— ∽ ——

At a quarter to ten, Holmes arrived with Inspector Peter Jones from the London police and a Mr. Merryweather, who was director of the City and Suburban Bank.

"This is the first Saturday night in twenty-seven years that I have missed my bridge game," grumbled Merryweather. "I do hope this is not some kind of wild goose chase."

Holmes grimaced. "This is a game you would hate

to lose, Mr. Merryweather. You stand to save at least thirty thousand pounds. And you may help catch John Clay, one of the most clever criminals in England."

"Indeed," agreed Inspector Jones, "Clay is known to be a thief, murderer, and forger. And he is slippery. Even though we haven't caught him yet, we've been tracing his crimes. Witnesses keep describing a thin man with a round scar on his forehead and pierced ears. One week we hear he has stolen some jewels, and the next week it is reported that he has arranged a murder and fake inheritance. His grandfather was a duke, and Clay earned college degrees at both Oxford and Cambridge."

"Well," said Holmes, "tonight his game is up. We'd best get to it."

We took two cabs and made our way to the same area Holmes and I had visited earlier that day. Merryweather led us from the gaslit street down a dark, narrow alley. He opened a side door to the City and Suburban Bank, and we entered a small passageway, using a lantern to light the way. This passage ended at a black wrought-iron gate, which Merryweather unlocked.

He then led us through another passageway that twisted and turned, until we went down some steps into a dank lower room. The lantern light flickered against the cold stone. Black spaces hid behind piled crates, and quivering shadows moved on the walls.

"What is in those crates?" I whispered.

"Gold coins," said Merryweather in a low voice.

"Thirty thousand gold napoleons borrowed from the French government."

While we were talking, Holmes went down on his knees to examine the cracks between the floor stones with the lantern and his magnifying glass. I could see now that he was looking for signs of a tunnel.

"Just as I suspected," he said quietly. "Clay and his friend Mr. Ross ought to make their move soon. They need only wait until the pawnbroker goes to bed. Mr. Jones, did you make the arrangements I requested?"

"Of course, Mr. Holmes," Jones replied, keeping his voice low. "There are three officers disguised and waiting near the front door of the pawnbroker's shop. If the criminals try to flee, they'll have no escape."

"Then we're ready," Holmes said, rising. "These men are dangerous, so I want everyone behind a crate. I'm going to cover the lantern with a screen. When I lift the screen, move in quickly. If there's a problem, don't hesitate to shoot."

We all took our positions, and Holmes covered the lantern. The darkness was complete, and the breathing of my companions seemed loud to my ears. My legs and knees grew sore from crouching, yet I dared not move lest I make a sound.

Suddenly, a thin beam of light shone through the cracks between the stones. I held my breath as it grew stronger and rumblings came from under the floor. Then, all at once, one of the stone slabs rose up, paused for a moment, and then fell back into place. Did the thieves know their plans had been discovered?

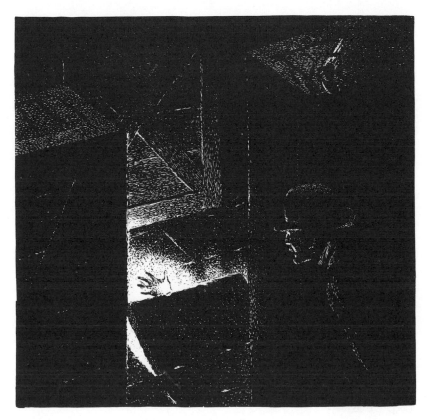

Nothing more happened for what seemed a very
long time. Then the stone again began to rise, and
this time it fell over and landed with a crash next to
my crate. A hand appeared in the light from the
tunnel and then a body. Wilson's clerk, still in his
suit, heaved himself up from the hole. "All's clear,
Archie," he whispered down. Then he bent to help a
slim man with bright red hair out of the hole.

Holmes didn't wait for the second man to fully
emerge. He leaped forward and grabbed Clay from
behind. "Give up, Clay," he shouted.

Clay's pistol glinted in the light, but the inspector's stick came down upon Clay's wrist, knocking the pistol to the floor. In the meantime Clay's partner threw himself back down the tunnel. His escape was in vain, however, because Inspector Jones's men were waiting for him at the other end.

In a moment Clay stopped struggling and straightened himself up, and Jones snapped handcuffs on him.

"Get your hands off of me," Clay said in a superior tone. "Do you forget that I am of royal blood?"

"Not at all, Your Grace," said the inspector, smiling triumphantly. "I'm ready to take you on a royal tour of Scotland Yard. And I am extremely grateful for the privilege."

Clay sneered and made a sweeping bow.

The inspector thanked Holmes and led Clay up the corridor. Sheepishly, Merryweather extended his hands to Holmes to thank him for saving the bank's gold napoleons.

"I'd say, Mr. Merryweather," said Holmes with a grin, "this was more exciting than any game of cards."

No one disagreed.

As you have seen, detective work sometimes means figuring out a crime before it is committed. Now that the notorious John Clay has been caught, we can look back and see how Sherlock Holmes managed to solve the case and catch the thieves in the act. Check the **CLUES** *to see if you followed all of Holmes's reasoning. When you're through, you'll be ready to join the master again the next time there's a mystery afoot!*

CLUES
that led to the solution of
The Redheaded League

 It is unusual for people to work for half wages if they can get full wages. Either the clerk is not very smart, thought Holmes, or he is very clever and has special reasons for wanting the pawnbroker's job. Holmes assumed it was the second explanation. The clerk must want to do something secret at the shop. This theory was strengthened by the fact that it was the clerk who had showed Wilson the advertisement for the Redheaded League and accompanied him to the interview. The clerk clearly wanted Wilson to take the job outside the shop.

 Wilson's description of the Redheaded League struck Holmes as very strange. What purpose could there be in copying pages from the *Encyclopaedia*? Therefore, Holmes thought the job with the Redheaded League must be a fake position. It was simply a way to keep Wilson out of his shop from ten o'clock to two o'clock each day. Holmes felt quite sure that something criminal must be going on at Wilson's shop while he was gone each day.

 When Wilson mentioned that his clerk had an acid scar on his forehead, Holmes thought immediately of the notorious criminal John Clay.

Clay had often been described in the newspapers. So
Holmes asked Wilson if his clerk had pierced ears.
Since Wilson replied that he did, Holmes thought it
was likely that Wilson's clerk was Clay. The question
then remained: What crime was Clay plotting to com-
mit this time?

Holmes thought the clerk's picture-taking habit
was odd. It could either be a way to catalog
everything in the pawnbroker's shop or an excuse
to go to the cellar. But what could be of interest in
the cellar? A tunnel was the most likely explanation.
This explanation was confirmed when Holmes saw the
stained and wrinkled knees of the clerk's trousers.
Obviously, the clerk had been busy digging on his knees.

If there were a tunnel, reasoned Holmes, it
could go toward the square, to a neighboring
house, or to something behind the shop. After
a look at the neighboring buildings, which were much
like Wilson's own, Holmes decided the tunnel was
probably leading somewhere else. So he tapped on
the pavement in front of the pawnshop and found that
it was solid. He knew then that there was no tunnel
going toward the square.

There was only one option left—the tunnel
must be headed for some place behind the shop.
So Holmes checked out the neighborhood and
found the bank. This was the most logical destination

for a criminal's tunnel. Holmes contacted the bank
and was told about the special treasure hoard in the
basement. Holmes knew then that he was right.

Since the Redheaded League had been dissolved,
Holmes knew the tunnel was finished. The
criminals no longer needed to keep Wilson out
of his shop. Holmes reasoned that the thieves would
seize upon the first possible evening to steal the gold,
so they wouldn't risk discovery. Their first chance
would come that evening, when the bank was closed
and the pawnbroker was asleep upstairs. If they
succeeded, they would have Sunday and Monday
to escape (since banks in England are closed on
Mondays). Holmes considered all this and made his
plan accordingly.

The Arms of the Worshipful Company of the Service

The Arms of The Worshipful Company of the Glaziers

The Arms of the Worshipful Company of Goldsmiths

The Arms of the Worshipful Company of Scriveners

The Arms of the Worshipful Company of Salters

The Arms of the Royal Company of Apothecaries

Inverness

Aberdeen

Storn

Dundee

Glasgow

BAKER

221

Regent's Park

Hampstead Road

Euston Rd.

City Road

York Road

Edgware Road

British Museum

Clerkenwell Rd.

221

Baker St.

Law Courts

Guildhall

Bishopsgate

Marylebone Road

Aldgate

Marble Arch

Piccadilly Circus

St Paul's Cathedral

b

Hyde Park

Bond St.

THE THAMES RIVER

Knightsbridge

Piccadilly

Blackfriars

Green Park

York

North Sea

St James

LONDON

Leeds

Hull

Irish Sea

Liverpool

Manchester

Stoke-on-Trent

a

The Adventure of
The Copper Beeches

HAMPSHIRE

Wolverhampton

Norwich

St. George's Channel

Birmingham

Northampton

Ipswich

b

The
Red headed League

FLEET STREET, LONDON

Hereford

Oxford

London

Cardiff

Bath

Tunbridge Wells

Taunton

Salisbury

a

Brighton

Dartmoor

Exeter

Bournemouth

Portsmouth

Plymouth

The Arms of the Honorable Company of East India Merchants

The Arms of the Honorable City of London

The ENGLAND
of Sherlock Holmes

The Arms of R's Shipping Company of Fortune Merchants

The Arms of R's Mercantile Company of English Merchants